Dear Parent:

Buckle up! You are about to join your child on a very exciting journey. The destination? Independent reading!

Road to Reading will help you and your child get there. The program offers books at five levels, or Miles, that accompany children from their first attempts at reading to successfully reading on their own. Each Mile is paved with engaging stories and delightful artwork.

Getting Started
For children who know the alphabet and are eager to begin reading
• easy words • fun rhythms • big type • picture clues

Reading With Help
For children who recognize some words and sound out others with help
• short sentences • pattern stories • simple plotlines

Reading On Your Own
For children who are ready to read easy stories by themselves
• longer sentences • more complex plotlines • easy dialogue

First Chapter Books
For children who want to take the plunge into chapter books
• bite-size chapters • short paragraphs • full-color art

Chapter Books
For children who are comfortable reading independently
• longer chapters • occasional black-and-white illustrations

There's no need to hurry through the Miles. Road to Reading is designed without age or grade levels. Children can progress at their own speed, developing confidence and pride in their reading ability no matter what their age or grade.

So sit back and enjoy the ride—every Mile of the way!

For Alison,
who appreciated
the silly things in life
E.W.

Library of Congress Cataloging-in-Publication Data
Weiss, Ellen, 1949-
New friend, blue friend / by Ellen Weiss ; illustrated by Larry DiFiori.
    p.   cm. — (Road to reading. Mile 2)
Summary: Splurge becomes attached to a fuzzy blue "friend" he
finds floating in the water and is unhappy when he cannot find it
one morning.
ISBN 0-307-26210-3
[1. Lost and found possessions—Fiction. 2. Monsters—Fiction.]
I. Di Fiori, Lawrence, ill.   II. Title.   III. Series.
PZ7.W4472Ne   1999   98-44158
                                                          CIP
                                                          AC

A GOLDEN BOOK • New York
Golden Books Publishing Company, Inc. New York, New York 10106

ISBN 0-307-26210-3   A MCMXCIX

New Friend, Blue Friend

by Ellen Weiss
illustrated by Larry DiFiori
MUPPET PRESS

It was a hot day
in the land of Ovadare.
Splurge was playing
in the water.
He kicked and splashed.

All of a sudden—SPLOOSH!
Something came
down the waterfall.
"Scary, scary!" said Splurge.

But it wasn't scary at all.

It looked like

a little blue monster.

It looked nice.

Splurge took it
out of the water.
He patted it dry.
"Hello!" he said to it.

But the little blue monster

did not answer.

"I will take him home
with me,"
Splurge said.
He named his friend Floofy.

11

At supper, Splurge gave Floofy
some of his pickle soup.

Floofy was not hungry.

At bedtime, Splurge let Floofy
share his cuddle rock.

"Do you want the
inside of the bed?"
asked Splurge.
"Or the outside?"

Floofy did not answer.
Splurge gave him the outside.

The next day,
Splurge took Floofy all over.
Floofy did not say much,
but he was nice.
He always listened to Splurge.

"Should we chase a butterfly?"
asked Splurge.

That was okay with Floofy.

"Do you like my funny hat?"
asked Splurge.
Floofy liked it just fine.

"Watch me spin!"
said Splurge.
Floofy watched and watched.
He never got bored.

Early one morning,
Floofy fell out of bed.

When Splurge got up,
he could not find Floofy
anywhere.

Splurge was worried.

He looked all over Ovadare.

Where could Floofy be?

"Aha!" said Splurge.

He pointed to a track
in the dirt.

"Floofy went that way!"

Splurge followed the tracks.
He went around and around,
but he didn't find Floofy.

At last, Splurge got
very, very dizzy.
He plopped down
on the ground.

And then, out of nowhere,
Floofy flew down
and bopped him on the nose!

"Floofy!" said Splurge.

"You can fly!"

He hugged Floofy.

"I am so happy you
came back," he said.

That night, Splurge and Floofy
had berry pie.

Then they listened to a story.

And after that,
Floofy stayed for good.